WICKED FIRE

A Paranormal Monster Romance

V. P. Nightshade

Sohmer Publishing

CONTENTS

COPYRIGHT

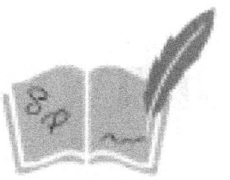

A BIG THANK YOU!

To My Readers ~
*Who are looking for something short
with a little more bite~*
*I look forward to reading
your reviews and comments!*

To Romana Disrud ~
Sometimes Wicked is just HOT!
Thanks for the title help!

As always, to that Grumpy Man ~
I'm glad you are still paying my bills!
I love you, baby!

WICKED FIRE

A DARK, ADDICTIVE MONSTER romance from author V. P. Nightshade.
For fans of obsession, erotic horror, and fated mates that burn the world down.

She wanted something real. She summoned something wicked.

Lonely and restless, tattoo artist Roxy Veil spends her nights chasing heat she can never hold on to. But when a mysterious stranger leaves behind a forbidden book, temptation calls louder than good sense. One reckless tattoo later, she awakens Izan—an ancient Ifrit made of fire, smoke, and devastating devotion.

Izan knows Roxy is his Sirati—the one woman fated to complete him. Her soul called him across realms. Her fear now threatens to destroy them both.

As an unnatural heatwave threatens to consume the city, Roxy must decide: resist the fire ... or let it claim her heart, her body, and her soul.

Dark. Addictive. Wickedly steamy.

One forbidden tattoo. One irresistible monster. Zero chance of walking away unscorched.

If you crave monster romance with fire-forged fated mates and molten passion, *Wicked Fire* will burn you alive—and make you beg for more.

Wicked Fire is a standalone, 20,000-word paranormal romance featuring a guarded tattoo artist, a seductive fire-djinn bound by fate, and a scorching fated-mates bond that ignites desire, danger, and redemption in the heart of a burning city.

No cliffhanger

No cheating

Just darkness, devotion, and one hell of a bite.

Part of the series **Fangs & Flesh: Short Monster Romance Tales.** Books in this series can be read in any order.

CONTENT & TRIGGER WARNINGS

WELCOME TO THE BURN.
This story isn't gentle.
It claws, it claims, and it ignites.

Wicked Fire is a paranormal romance filled with passion, primal longing, and supernatural heat that scorches far beyond the skin. The following content warnings are offered to ensure readers can make informed choices before entering Roxy Veil's inferno.

This novella contains:

- **Steamy content** and detailed erotic scenes involving consent-driven primal dynamics and supernatural intimacy

- **Supernatural themes** involving summoning, fated mates, elemental magic, fire symbolism, and ancient soul-bonding

- **Psychological trauma** related to abandonment, betrayal, and emotional loss

- **Past emotional abuse** and theft from a former partner (non-graphic but impactful)

- **Grief and loss** from the death of a parent (referenced in memory)

- **Apocalyptic imagery** including intense heat, fire, collapsing infrastructure, and citywide unrest

- **Sensory overload** depictions (heat-induced hallucinations, dreamlike eroticism, bodily reactions to magical stimuli)

- **Monster romance themes** involving a fire-being (Ifrit) and human heroine, including intense romantic/sexual bonding

- **Profanity and dark humor** used throughout for tone and characterization

Reader Notes:

This is a high-heat, fated-mates romance with emotional bite and poetic prose. The story leans into the monstrous, the mythic, and the mythically horny. If you enjoy your love interests smoldering—literally—and your heroines emotionally scarred but defiant, *Wicked Fire* was written for you.

You won't find cheating or cliffhangers here.

But you will find ash, devotion, and the kind of touch that brands.

Enter at your own desire. And don't forget to bring water.

EPIGRAPH

Wicked Fire

When Roxy Veil first touched the flame,
She didn't know it had a name.
A Rune etched deep in aching skin
Became the spark that drew him in.

Her inked rebellion, sharp and wild,
Was longing scrawled in heat defiled.
She called for love, for pain, for more—
And something ancient split the door.

From smoke and shadow, flame took shape,
A god half-bound by fate and ache.
Izan rose with molten grace—
A fire with a human face.

He saw her fear, her hard disguise,
The bruised rebellion in her eyes.
But fire knows what coldness hides—
And melts the steel where shame resides.

She fought the burn, denied the brand,
But still, he waited—heart in hand.
For even flames that scorch and sear
Can be a cure for frozen fear.

And when she broke—when walls gave way,
She chose the fire. Let it stay.
Their bodies blazed, their souls entwined,
A bond no ash would ever bind.

So let the world forget the cold,
Let rain kiss embers growing bold—
For love like theirs, once set alight,
Is forged in dark...
and burns through night.

~V. P. Nightshade
Read by the Author
   https://youtu.be/wAr_TM6aKs4

ASHES AND INK

THE FLUORESCENT LIGHTS FIZZED and hummed, drowning the shop in a yellow haze that only made its shadows darker. Roxy Veil closed the heavy glass door and watched her ghost reflection linger there before shivering out of sight. She felt as though she were dissolving just as easily as her reflection; melting into the thick heat of *Veil and Ink* where she stayed long after hours, the fans struggling to cool her restless skin. The shop smelled of metal and lemon soap, ink and want. As she wiped down her station, every brush of her rag against the counter was a challenge she threw at the empty air: look how fine I am without you.

The silence inside *Veil and Ink* wrapped around Roxy like gauze—thick, sterile. A breath caught in the lungs of the world. She glanced toward the front window where the evening light slashed through blinds, gilding the worn hardwood floors.

The scent of lemon oil and eucalyptus air freshener brought the memories back—too fast, too much.

Roxy's father had abandoned her mother when Roxy was a baby. She couldn't even remember him.

Her mom had been a quiet woman with steel in her bones. The two were close, but her mother always warned her: *"You give too much away, Roxy. You bleed love and expect people not to drown."*

It had been four years since her mother died. Cancer. The kind that took everything except the time to say goodbye.

Roxy inherited a small insurance payout, an old Toyota, and a diamond encrusted locket her mother never took off. She sold the locket to help put a down payment on the building. The car—well, Evan stole that. Along with the ten grand in their joint savings account she kept for emergencies, and the last fragile piece of her heart she hadn't yet walled off.

They had been high school sweethearts, and he was her first everything.

For over a year after her mother had died, Evan acted like a partner—helping her with renovation decisions for *Veil and Ink*, encouraging her to follow her dream, pretending to be her rock. She could still see the tattoo machine he bought for her 25th birthday that first year. Said it meant he believed in her art, in her dream.

He'd made promises for the future, marriage and their own little family.

Liar.

He'd kissed her that night like a promise, then a month later, kissed her goodbye without a word. No note. No confrontation. Just silence—their savings account wiped out and an empty parking space where her mother's car used to be.

The police shrugged, called it a civil matter. She'd admitted that she frequently allowed him to drive the car and of course there were *"No signs of forced entry."*

The bank shrugged. "He had access. The account was in his name, too."

Everyone shrugged, except her.

The pain was severe. The humiliation was worse.

The betrayal crippled the business. For a while she tattooed in half-dark, hardly ate or slept, couldn't afford proper cooling, did all her own branding and booking.

She didn't speak to anyone about it — not even Raven, the goth girl she had hired, her biggest defender and who had over time become her best friend. Her only friend.

Roxy worked to wall off her heart and rebrand herself with sarcasm, ink, and solitude.

She'd stopped bleeding about it a long time ago. Now she just protected herself as much as she could because she understood that trusting a man meant ruin.

Three years later and she had only started dating. If going to the bar and picking up a nameless stranger for sex in the hourly motel could be called dating.

Her body was open; her heart never was.

She sighed and mentally shook herself.

She organized her tattoo machines with sharp precision, building her loneliness into towers of immaculate control. Her heart pounded as she replayed the quiet refrain of another upcoming empty night.

She wiped a fresh smear of ink off her thigh, grimacing as the rag caught on a ripped thread from her jean shorts. With every snap of a lid and click of a case, she felt a little more like a woman closing the door on her own desires — maybe, this time, they'd stay shut.

But who the fuck was she kidding? She was restless, a house with no one home, heat lightning with no rain. She set her mouth in a determined line and cursed under her breath, wishing the night away.

She wiped her brow with the back of an ink-stained hand and decided she needed a drink.

Or a stranger.

Or maybe just a week of cold showers.

Roxy never got the chance to hate the silence — Raven Morrow, her other artist, strolled in with her black lips, eyeliner, and pierced tongue, trailing spicy-sweet aromatic cigarette smoke like a war flag.

"If I have to tattoo one more basic bitch asking for a butterfly, I'm going to stab myself with my own needle." Raven's voice cut through the room, sharp and startling. She lounged against the counter like a cat with nothing to prove, a clove cigarette balanced on her lip, watching Roxy's shift-ending ritual with the smallest hint of amusement.

Roxy exhaled a breath she didn't know she'd been holding and gave her friend a sidelong glance. "Only if I can watch."

"You'd be lost without me, Veil," Raven said with a smile. Her boots made a low thud on the floor as she moved closer and leaned against the wall beside the sterilizer cabinet. "Half those trust-fund rebels wouldn't last five seconds in here without a free therapy session from me."

They fell into silence again, the easy kind born of long hours and quiet trust. The fans spun lazily above, doing little to push back the humid weight in the room. Outside, the city throbbed with distant sirens and bass-heavy music. Inside, the shop buzzed with silence and heat.

"It's fucking boiling out there. Pretty sure I saw some guy hallucinating a My Little Pony on his way to the bus stop." Raven flicked ash into an empty soda can with a flick of her black-polished thumbnail. She tilted her head to watch the smoke spiral upward. "What the hell are you still doing here, anyway? I thought you were going to go out and get your groove on."

Roxy shrugged, jaw tight. "You know me," she said, picking up a needle and inspecting it for invisible flaws. "Living the dream."

Raven raised a skeptical eyebrow, reaching for the whiskey hidden behind a row of inks. She poured two generous shots and slid one across the counter. "If this is your dream, I'm scared to ask what your nightmares look like."

Roxy downed the drink, setting the glass down harder than she meant. "Nothing I can't handle."

"You're going to die of boredom if the heat doesn't kill you first," she muttered.

Roxy smirked, but didn't look up. "Bold of you to assume I haven't been dead inside for years."

Raven exhaled dramatically. "Same, but at least I make it fashion." Smoke curled lazily around the metal ring in her nose. "Anymore walk-ins while I was gone, or did the sweat scare 'em off?"

"Usual crowd," Roxy answered, sweeping a strand of burgundy hair out of her eyes. "Couple of college kids thinking they're edgy. A bridal party who left as soon as I said I don't do discount daisies."

"You see that guy earlier?" Raven asked finally, voice softer, curious. "Came in, didn't say much. Book under his arm. Creepy as hell. The one that was nosing around and looking at the tattoo example books when I went to dinner? Looked like he was your type. You know. Not." Raven gave a playful laugh.

Roxy hesitated. That man had felt ... wrong. Or right, in a way that made her skin crawl with awareness. "He was just looking."

"Uh-huh. He left something behind, you know. A skeevy book. Looks like it crawled out of a forbidden section of a haunted library."

Raven pushed a weathered, leather-bound book across the counter. It looked ancient—edges frayed, cover cracked, faint scorch marks etched across the front like old claw wounds.

Roxy raised a brow. "You didn't burn this yourself with a smudge stick and good intentions?"

Raven snorted. "Bitch, I haven't saged anything since I set my laundry on fire."

The joke failed to register as Roxy inspected the book.

Her fingers skimmed the surface of the book with interest. It felt warm. Too warm. As if it had life.

"What kind of guy just leaves something like this behind?" she murmured, flipping through its heavy pages. Her voice had the hunger of a girl who'd spent too many nights with no one to talk to.

"A weird, creepy, silent dude, that's who. Book looks like some kind of goth breadcrumb from a horror movie that comes with a curse and a soundtrack." Raven said, teeth closing around the butt of her cigarette as smoke escaped her mouth. "But looks like he found your kink. You think he was trying to impress you with this,

Veil?" Raven snorted, raising a brow as she leaned in for a better look. "I know you like 'em weird, but this little gift is next-level shit."

Her voice jolted Roxy out of the fog she'd been in since the man walked through her door earlier, since he'd left her with more questions than customers. She ran her hands over the book's cracked leather cover, fingertips brushing dust and mystery off its surface. She held the volume between herself and Raven like a fragile secret, the spine strangely warm to the touch.

Roxy hummed in response, but didn't look up as she flipped through the first few pages, words, and symbols inside like nothing she'd ever seen, and like everything she'd ever needed.

They throbbed like ink still wet.

Raven shrugged, blowing smoke out of the corner of her mouth. "It really looks like a spell book. Maybe he's planning to come back for it? Or you?" Her tone was teasing, but the way her eyes lingered on Roxy spoke of other worries. "If you summon sexy demons from that thing, I'm quitting," she said, drumming her fingers against the counter. "And I'm telling everyone I warned you. Some books should stay closed, boss." Raven continued, looking at the pictures on the pages with very little interest.

Roxy's eyes remained on the book, the edges of her vision tinged with the raw, strange glow of symbols too old for her world. "You're such a bitch." She murmured.

"And you're too hot to stay home every night. Just sayin'." Raven said, grabbing her sunglasses, watching Roxy's fascination with a mixture of amusement and disbelief. "I'm out. Don't summon Satan without me. I have some questions for that fucker! See you in the a.m."

Roxy let out a short, sharp laugh, running her fingers over the sketchbook, flipping through the pages. She could feel its heat through the thick leather, burning with lines she had only dared imagine. Designs that said more than any lover ever had.

Roxy waved and watched Raven leave; the door swinging closed behind her, then looked back down at the book.

The book was more than old. Its ancient, cracked leather breathed secrets into her hands. She flipped another page, feeling its weight like a promise she was too needy to express. The words seemed alive, pulsing and shifting in ways ink never should.

"I can't believe he just forgot this," Roxy whispered to herself.

Roxy turned another page, more brittle parchment, more symbols she couldn't name. It called to her, not with words, but with the muted insistence of something ordained. The letters twisted under the fluorescent lights, promising secrets she had no right to understand.

The lights buzzed, one flickering before sputtering back to life. She kept flipping through the pages, scanning the runes and diagrams, tracing them with careful fingertips. The sensation was electric, making her shiver even in the humid night.

The book seemed to glow brighter, burning just enough to be tempting, just enough to sear. *Demons?* She shook her head and laughed, but the sound was swallowed by the thickening air. "Wouldn't be the first time I've made a terrible decision," Roxy murmured.

***

Locking up the shop, Roxy settled into the quiet, feeling it rise around her in layers she couldn't peel back. The shop was an island in the city's noise, the muted sounds of cars and late-night life almost gone now, swallowed by the humid air and the pulse of her own breathing. Her mind buzzed with fragments of thoughts, too scattered to follow and too loud to ignore. She glanced around the room, the yellow lights flickering, the corners pooling in darkness, the scent of ink and heat-treated leather mingling with the remains of Raven's cigarette smoke. It should have felt empty, this space she owned, but instead it felt like everything she'd spent years refusing to fill was about to crash into her all at once.

She was restless.

And horny.

She thought once again about going down to the pub and picking up something strange; as long as he was muscled and hard enough to take the edge off.

Then she moved once again to the counter as if she couldn't help herself.

She stared at the book, the thickness of it, the weight of what it offered. Her hands hovered above the spine before she picked it up again, savoring the heat that spread through her palms. Roxy felt the heat in her chest, her throat, the base of her spine. She closed her eyes against the dizzying rush and let it sink in, knowing she couldn't fight it even if she wanted to. And she didn't want to. Not tonight.

The surrounding room contracted and expanded with the ragged rhythm of her thoughts, and Roxy let herself sink deeper into its warm oblivion. The fans spun slow above her, casting shadows that flickered across her skin. The stillness seemed alive, charged with the urgency of her own heart. She poured another shot of whiskey and held the glass, the coolness in stark contrast to the feverish fire that danced beneath her fingers and within her veins.

She flipped through the pages again, each one more tempting, each one like a breathless secret only she could unravel. The pages seemed endless, full of shapes and designs that promised more than art, more than skin-deep lines. She didn't know what any of it meant, but she could feel its truth. It was an invitation, the kind she never received and always longed for. She needed it. She needed to give in, give over, let herself want this, this one thing that no one else had the power to take away.

She reached another page, and her breath caught in her throat.

There, sprawled across two facing pages, was a rune. Circular. Twisting. Its edges flared like smoke licking up a matchstick. The center spiraled inward, coiling like a snake made of fire. She blinked. It almost looked like it breathed.

Heat bloomed low in her belly.

The design seemed to move, to pulse with a life and light that wasn't quite ink and wasn't quite anything she'd ever seen. A spiral of flame and thorns, bold and fierce and alive. Beneath it, scrawled in a slanted, ink-faded hand, were two words etched like a warning or a promise: *Lurian Sigil.* Just below, in finer script—so faint it looked like smoke pressed into parchment—*For love, for devotion, for forever. Where longing burns, so shall he come.*

It was more than a design. It was a promise. A promise she wanted to believe in.

Her lips formed the question. "What's the worst that could happen?" she whispered. "You already gave your love to a thief. Let's see what happens when you give your skin to magic."

It was a dare. She threw back another drink and felt it settle warm and dangerous in her stomach, a twin to the sensation of the book in her hand.

The lights dimmed around her, the room narrowing until the book was the only thing she saw. Her head spun with the thrill of discovery, the fear of what it meant, the need to find out. She touched the page; the ink warming her fingertips, breathing life into her empty places. Her thoughts collided with the alcohol in a dizzying mess of desire and doubt; fear and exhilaration. She had to do it.

Roxy reached for her tattoo pen, hands steady, mind wild, breath quick, and resolve solid. She felt the air change around her, heavy and thick with heat and hope.

The thrill of risk tingled across her skin.

***

The book lay open, its presence a demanding whisper against her resolve. She glanced at the page; the rune glowed with a promise she was ready to believe.

The tattoo machine buzzed to life in Roxy's hand, its familiar hum vibrating through her bones and settling in the depths of her belly.

The sound filled the silence of the shop, louder now that the world outside had slipped away. She was alone, finally and truly alone, her skin hungry for what the book offered. Her thigh was bare, skin exposed and eager.

The first touch of the needle sent a shockwave through her, raw and consuming. It was fire and heat, a flash of hissing pain tempered with something sweeter. She gripped the pen machine tighter, lips parted in surprise as the sensation dug deeper than ink and skin. Roxy rode the edge between fear and excitement, the world narrowing to the tattoo and what it would become. Her pulse matched the beat of the needle, quick and insistent.

This was how it felt to take risks, to surrender control.

This was how it felt to be alive.

The pain mingled with a reckless joy she hadn't let herself feel in years, a sensation she thought she'd buried alongside her needs. The air grew thick and intimate, the shop closing in on her as if to hold her steady. Sweat trickled down her back, and the ink glowed copper beneath her skin.

The design pulsed as if alive.

Her breath caught and stuttered in her throat as she worked. The air thickened around her, an intimate embrace that pulled her further from the world she knew and closer to the truth she dared to want. She didn't pause, didn't think, just followed the lines of the rune as it took form beneath her skin. The familiar vibration of the tattoo pen seemed to change, the resonance deeper, reaching into the secret places she never showed.

The fans struggled to move the heavy air as she drew ink into her skin. Sweat dampened the edges of her resolve, but not enough to stop her.

Besides, she didn't know how to stop, didn't know if she ever wanted to.

The ink glowed faintly, alive and breathing.

Her vision blurred, her senses collided, but the tattoo was a lifeline, a promise she wouldn't let go.

Roxy was sweat-slicked and ink-stained, a beautiful, broken chaos. Her body sang with heat and effort, a hum of desperation that wouldn't leave her alone.

Her skin drank in the ink. The need, the thrill of finally risking it all.

The tattoo emerged like a revelation, like a secret only she was meant to uncover. She didn't let herself think beyond the next line, the next breath, the next rush of sensation that carried her higher.

By the time the final thorned curl sealed the spiral, her breath was coming in shallow bursts. The rune glowed. Not with magic, she told herself—but with blood, adrenaline, madness.

The lights above her buzzed. Dimmed. Went still.

Something inside the walls thrummed — slow and low, like a heartbeat.

Roxy's fingers trembled around the pen tattoo machine.

And from the shadows behind her, the air warmed.

THE MARK THAT BURNS

THE RUNE ON HER thigh pulsed like a second heartbeat.

Roxy sat frozen in the center of the shop, tattoo gun still humming beside her, the metallic tang of blood and ink sharp in the thick air. Her breath came fast, shallow. The fans overhead spun uselessly, the blades clunking as though they too were suffocating.

The room felt wrong. Not just hot — alive. Watching.

Her legs were still bare on the rolling chair, her shorts rumpled on the floor where she had left them after closing up. She touched the tattoo gingerly and felt it throb in time with her pulse.

Ink hadn't hurt like this since she was eighteen, since her skin was new and she didn't know yet what she could stand. Now it burned. Like a live flame. She whispered a curse as heat licked at the back of her neck and the overhead lights flickered like dying stars, signaling another possible brownout due to the unusual summer heat.

Am I having a reaction to my own ink? Did I have too much to drink? One too many shots of whiskey?

She yanked her shorts back on, shivering despite the July heat.

"Okay, not normal," she muttered. "Not normal."

The shop was too quiet. Too still. The chairs waited in silence. Her tattoo guns sat like weapons resting before a war. Even the lemon soap and sweat clinging to her skin felt heavier, sharper.

The rune pulsed.

But beneath the silence, something unfamiliar needled its way in. Unease. A low thrum building in her gut and rising to meet the metallic tang now spreading across her tongue.

Roxy took a breath, trying to steady her heart, ignoring the growing sense that the room had become something predatory. Heat kissed the small of her back with rough insistence. She touched the tattoo again and winced. It felt increasingly like a mistake.

An indulgence she'd dared herself into. An indulgence that got you burned.

The shop seemed to hold its breath; like it had twisted just slightly out of shape. She stood. Her breath came quick. The air tasted coppery. The lights dimmed. Reality warped just a little. Her boots scuffed the concrete floor as she crossed the room.

The sound startled her in the oppressive quiet, and she jumped. Now, even her breathing seemed loud in the dead air.

Roxy squeezed her eyes shut. *You've got to be fucking kidding. There is no reason to be freaking out like this!*

When she opened them, the shop wavered like a mirage. She stumbled back, her thigh alive with a fresh blaze of pain. *All right, all right. Not normal.* She gritted her teeth against the burn, against the sudden memory of waking up alone, betrayed and abandoned; after her last fucked-up mistake.

No. This is my shop. My world. Whatever this is, it won't last. It's just a mirage caused by the overwhelming heat. The alcohol. A trick of my imagination.

Even telling herself that, her pulse hammered at her, thrumming like a second heartbeat against the confusion and doubt.

No, she thought again, with more defiance than certainty. *I'm not afraid of anything I can't touch.*

***

Roxy moved to clean up her station, hoping the motion would break the oppressive stillness of the shop and take her mind off the ache in her thigh. Her hands were traitors, trembling and unsure, belying the calm she pretended to feel. She reached for the metal tray of tattoo tools.

The tray shimmered.

Roxy stared.

It didn't reflect her face. The surface rippled. Smoke curled upward, soft and seductive. The scent of gas and scorched metal filled her lungs. Her heartbeat thundered. Her breath hitched.

The tray rattled against the counter, vibrating with a strange, terrifying purpose.

She stared, unblinking, while the room blurred around her. Her heartbeat was deafening. Her breathing quickened, shallow and afraid. The air filled with the acrid smell of burnt offerings and ozone, leaving her breathless with its intensity.

"Fine, then. Just keep ignoring it," she said to herself, but her voice shook as much as her body. Her instincts screamed on the raw edge of panic, warning her to run. She pretended not to hear, waging a silent battle against the tide of something larger than she had ever felt.

The trembling got worse. She gripped the tray and her skin burned where it brushed the metal. She imagined her fear etched into it, imagined the heat cutting like a fresh line of ink across her bones.

For once, she wished she believed in something enough to pray to it.

Her muscles strained as the ground tilted and the surrounding walls contracted. Her breath came faster. The uncertainty of what was happening slipped through her mind like quicksilver, and still, she fought against knowing. She clung to denial, to defiance, with a grip that threatened to break her.

The metal surface shimmered in the half-light, showing the impossible.

Steel and tools fell to the floor with a clatter as she dropped the tray, falling back against her chair, her eyes wide as she watched the universe unwind itself. The steel warped and liquefied. It moved with liquid purpose, forming the outline of something else. The surrounding space blurred, a violent edge of colors and sound, blending the real with the surreal.

Nothing made sense as the shop sang with energy.

She watched, unable to tear her eyes away.

Smoke curled upward from the tray, claiming the air with soft and sultry insistence. It bloomed, rising around her like an echo, like an unwanted memory, teasing at the edges of her vision and her mind. It touched her with the lightest of hands. Her breathing turned shallow, ragged. Her blood thundered in her ears, drowning out thought.

Her heartbeat. The only sound. The last sound.

It embodied everything she had ever refused to believe in. She reached for something, anything, but found nothing she could hold. She wanted to laugh and scream at once, feeling both more alive and more terrified than ever before. Her thoughts broke apart, scattering like the glowing smoke, but she held on with raw, defiant need.

This was her shop, her body, her life. This was her fear, her panic, her breath catching in her throat.

She choked on the taste of metal. On the sour burn of ozone and disbelief.

She told herself it wasn't real. It was a hallucination. She wouldn't believe it.

As the lines between the worlds bled together, a soundless cry tore itself from her lips. Her head snapped back, and the room spun, stretching around her like an artist's dark dream. The heat of her rune blistered against her skin. Her fingers were weak as they traced the mark on her thigh.

The words came out in a whisper, finally conceding.

"Oh god," Roxy said. "I believe it."

***

From the metal spilled across the floor, a shadow unfolded. Long limbs. Broad shoulders. Heat radiated in waves from the center, curling the air, blistering the edges of her breath.

Roxy cringed, primal and panicked. It was an animal's instinct, blind and involuntary; reacting to imminent danger and knowing that it was already too late to escape.

She backed toward the wall, mouth dry. "No. No fucking way."

The smoke had merged into a single being – molten and mighty. A creature of fire stretched into her world with deliberation and grace, like a god enjoying his creation. He was bare-chested and barefoot. Bronze-skinned, hard-muscled and taller than any man she'd ever seen. His eyes burned gold with promise — lit from within like twin suns behind a veil of storm. His hair coiled like black-smoke, flickering at the ends as if the air refused to cool him. Tattoos marked his arms in ink and ember, coiling and shifting like smoke under the skin. The heat of him was a physical force, pressing hard against the boundaries of what Roxy could endure. Wherever he stepped, the wood floor blackened, a scar marking his path.

Roxy's breath caught. Her mind shattered.

He was impossible. And utterly real.

Then he spoke. "Sirati. You called ... and I have come."

The voice was smoke and sand, thunder rolled low across desert stone for an eternity. It vibrated through her bones, not loud but true—as if it belonged to her.

She stumbled away from him. Her thigh flared with heat. The rune burned in recognition.

The smoke curled around his frame as if worshipping him. He was beauty made dangerous, devotion made flesh.

He stepped closer.

The world condensed. Nothing mattered except this act of fiery creation. This impossible reality. His power was vast and ancient and so close she could almost touch it; feel it hot and heavy against her skin.

Roxy trembled where she stood, a collision of panic and awe and unending shock. She was powerless to stop any of it; but the sight of him filled her with unfamiliar warmth. Not just warmth. Desire. Hot need. She had opened herself up to this moment, to this terrible wonder, and she knew it would consume her. Her heart slammed against her chest. Against her control. Nothing was solid anymore, except for the flare of her rune and the gold of his eyes and the heat of him.

So much heat.

His entire being smoldered, skin still shimmering with his fading heat. Faint wisps of gold ash rose from his shoulders—but the glow was dimming, retreating inward like embers losing breath.

Roxy's fear flared bright, sharp as kindling, only to dissolve into something that threatened to unravel her.

She felt raw and open.

Small, against the burning weight of him.

He was both more and less than she had ever dreamed. A creature of fire and sensuality and pure molten light.

This isn't real. I need to go to the hospital. This is a fucking bad reaction. The thoughts flew through her mind with the speed of light.

She swallowed and asked, "Who?"

He stepped forward. The floor beneath his bare feet hissed softly. A faint scorch mark bloomed beneath his heel.

"I am Izan, my Sirati." His voice was deep and smoky and purely sexual. "And you ..." His gaze flicked to her thigh. The rune. "... are mine."

Izan moved with feral grace, as if the shop were nothing but a backdrop for his presence. For his perfection. The cooling heat radiated from his body in waves, palpable and urgent, leaving Roxy dizzy and overwhelmed.

"The fuck I am," she whispered.

He tilted his head slightly, not angered — amused. Curious. Reverent.

"You called me. You marked yourself. I came. For you."

"This isn't real. You're not real. I — I drank too much. I am having a reaction. This is a dream, or a breakdown, or—"

"You know better." His voice rolled over her like distant thunder. Like a promise. The air between them sparked with connection.

She stared in disbelief; desperate and longing for something she couldn't name. This was not real. It couldn't be. She didn't want it to be. She wanted. Well, she didn't know what she wanted anymore, but this was more than she could stand. More than she could survive. The rune on her thigh burned — not painfully, but insistently. Like a tether being pulled.

The certainty that this would undo her was written in every line of her skin and every thrum of her heart. She forced her eyes shut, hoping he would disappear. Hoping he wouldn't. When she opened them again, he was still there. Bright and dark and alive.

Izan was close now, almost close enough to touch her, close enough that she could feel his heat shimmer against her skin. Close enough to steal her words and her will.

Her rune pulsed with need.

Her heart beat too fast. Her skin flushed. The ache low in her belly told her exactly what this was, even though her mind refused to believe it.

She took a step back, then another. The wooden paneling on the wall met her spine with rough indifference.

The way he looked at her was unbearable. The way he looked at her was everything.

The temperature rose in her body, leaving Roxy breathless and trembling and overwhelmed with panic and desire. Mostly desire. The room spun. Her mind spun. Her whole life spun, bright as the arc of a shooting star, a trail of ash and flame and inevitability. She was caught in the orbit of him, and there was no escaping.

Not when she saw herself in his endless, golden, unbreakable gaze.

***

Roxy pressed back against the wall. Her breath hitched. She was terrified. She was trapped, caught between fear and an inexplicable, primal attraction. The breathless heat that spread through her had nothing to do with the temperature.

"Who the hell are you?" she demanded again, her voice raw and louder than she intended.

Izan stepped closer, fluid and restrained. "Yours." One word, simple with the weight of eternity.

Roxy's back was slick with sweat and disbelief as the world narrowed around her. The rune on her thigh pulsed, hot and intimate. Her body ached with confusion and need as she stood frozen in his intense gaze.

His presence left her dizzy. Consumed. There was no room for anything but him, but she tried to convince herself that he wasn't real. She tried, and she failed. Roxy's mind refused to stop spinning, careening between panic and desire.

Heat saturated the shop, but it paled compared to the inferno consuming her. She needed space to breathe, but the air was thick and filled with the scent of smoke and ash and his vivid form.

He moved closer. His footsteps were measured and confident, never doubting, never hesitating. Like he knew her.

"Stop," she said, throwing a hand out to protect herself, her voice almost breaking. Almost betraying her.

He stopped. Just stood there, radiant and still, like a god waiting for permission. His smoke black hair moved in the drafts from the fans above, like the smoke that had formed him, and Roxy's thoughts shifted like flame, flickering from clarity to chaos and back again.

The air vibrated. The ground beneath her feet felt ready to give way, but she held her ground with defiant intensity.

She glared at him, trying to be stronger than she felt, trying to push away everything but logic. "You've got the wrong girl. I didn't call anyone."

"Yes," he said. "You did." His words were a sacred vow, tender and immovable. "My spark. You called, you conjured, and I am bound to you."

Roxy shivered, heat pooling low in her stomach. A molten weight that left her weak and wanting. Her own words came back to her, mocking and true. *Not normal. Not normal.* The room spun, and she was left with nothing but her own breath and his infinite, waiting eyes.

A wave of heat pulsed from the rune, insistent and all-consuming, leaving Roxy shaking, raw and open to him. Her fingers skimmed the curve of her thigh — heat pulsed there, sharp and fevered — making sure the tattoo was real. And in turn, that she was real, too.

Under his gaze, she swore the secrets she'd buried deep beneath bone and breath lit up like kindling, exposed for him to read and know all.

It terrified her.

The longer she looked at him, the harder it was to tear her gaze away. The harder it was to pretend that this was just an infectious fever dream.

Roxy clung to her skepticism with all her might, but her might was dwindling.

I conjured him???

She didn't know how to handle this. How to handle him.

She had opened herself to this, dared herself into it, and now there was no escape. Only him. Only her. The rising temperature claimed her.

His obvious devotion and presence claimed her even more.

"Fuck," she said, because there was nothing else she could say. Nothing else that would hold. Her certainty shattered, and she was left with an unbearable, exquisite need.

Roxy touched the Rune on her thigh. It burned beneath her fingers, not with pain, but with awakening.

With recognition.

Her voice broke. "I didn't mean to."

"But you did." His voice wrapped around her like smoke. "And now, Roxy, my Sirati ... I am yours."

BOUND BY FIRE

THE SMOKE DIDN'T CLEAR. It clung.

It wound around the chairs and coiled beneath the counter like it belonged there, like it had always been there, waiting. The overhead lights flickered once—twice—before surrendering to the heat with a final, wheezing pop. Roxy stood in the darkened silence of *Veil and Ink,* her breath shallow, the rune on her thigh pulsing like a second, molten heart.

He hadn't moved since he'd spoken her name.

Izan.

He stood in the center of her shop, feet bare on hardwood that smoked faintly beneath his weight. Bronze skin glistened in the soft orange glow bleeding from his body, sweat, or something else, catching the low light that filtered in from the street. His muscles were carved with precision, his chest moving gently with every breath. The ember runes on his body moved like living flame, and his golden eyes didn't stray from hers.

Roxy's heart thundered a denial even her lips wouldn't voice. She moved to the side, tripping over the detritus of the shop. A tray of tattoo needles hit the floor, clattering, spreading like spilled secrets.

The sound didn't faze him.

"This can't be happening," she muttered, eyes wide, seeing not the monster she'd expected but something more terrifying—someone who looked at her like he had been waiting forever; like a worshiper might watch fire—reverent, patient, deadly if misused.

"What the fuck are you?" she whispered, throat dry. Roxy's instincts shrieked, a chorus of flight and fight and desperate confusion. She swallowed, finding no relief in the dry air. Her mind was a splintered reel, stuck on how, why and why now.

Izan stepped forward. Slowly. Deliberately. Each footfall leaving a ghost of smoke. When Izan stopped, his golden eyes pinned her to the spot with an intimacy that stripped her bare.

Predatory. Knowing. They narrowed as though she was the one consuming him.

His voice, when it came, was rough silk and broken vows. "Ashling, you marked yourself."

She flinched as he spoke, her shoulder hitting the shelf behind her. Bottles rattled. The shop was too hot. She could taste metal on her tongue, like she'd been sucking on copper wire.

He approached slowly, molten and relentless, until the world was nothing but the burn of him.

"You called me," he said. "With your want. Your ink. Your ache," he said, reverent, brutal in his simplicity. "I am what you made me. Your need called me. Your lovely hands made me flesh."

Her mind spun, and her body betrayed it with every traitorous throb where the rune inked her thigh.

"Bullshit," she shot back, but even that word seemed to sear the air. She fought for control, his heat like a brand against everything she'd walled off. She could see it in the set of his jaw, the curve of his shoulder: he was as beautiful as he was inevitable. "That's not — That's not how this works."

His eyes softened, molten pools threaded with smoke. "It is. The void was vast. I have waited lifetimes for you to call me from it. You wrote my mark into yourself, Sirati. We are bound. I am yours." Each word pulsed like a drumbeat, deep and ritualistic.

She looked down. Her thigh throbbed—deep, steady. The rune glowed faintly, a heartbeat she couldn't deny.

"This is insane," she whispered, choking on the smoke of it all. The air was electric with his presence. Roxy's skin tingled, her heart jack-hammered, and the shop seemed far too small for everything happening inside it. "I was drunk. I was lonely. It means nothing."

"It means everything," he said simply.

She retreated further, trying to will her breath steady. Her back hit the corner, giving her nowhere else to go. Then she suddenly remembered Raven's words and blurted out, "Are you a demon?"

"No, my spark! I am an Ifrit." Izan told her softly.

"An If — What?" She asked.

"An Ifrit. A djinn of fire. A magical being. There are many of us. But, I assure you, I am not a demon. I would never harm you. I am yours."

"And what, you just expect me to believe that?" She demanded, hoping the bite in her tone masked the tremble.

Izan's eyes softened, but the intensity remained. "Believe, or not," he replied, the patience of centuries weighing each syllable. "Our bond does not depend on your faith, only your heart." He paused, a visible hunger there—need, but also something deeper. "You drew me to your world, Roxy. To you. Deny me, and the magic of the universe will respond. Deny its gifts and the world will burn with you."

She blinked at him, and something about the way he looked at her—like she was precious, like she was dangerous—twisted the ache in her chest. "I thought you said you would never hurt me!"

"I would never. But your own actions can harm you." His was the calm voice of reason.

"I didn't ask for this," she said.

"No," Izan murmured, "but you needed it."

Her defiance flared like the heat she was choking on. "Oh yeah? Why would I even want you?" she said, and there it was—naked, raw, the fear in every brutal syllable.

For a moment he let her words create space and then he exhaled, a breath that seemed to scorch his lungs before it reached the air. He continued to watch her: complete, unending, like she was her own answer.

"Ask yourself," he murmured.

The rune throbbed beneath her skin, matching the pounding in her skull. Her mind swirled with impossibilities, terror coiled with a desire she'd caged and branded and never once let free. She looked at him, into him, the creature who claimed that she made him flesh, standing real and full of fire and the promise of something more.

The heat was unbearable. Her shirt clung to her skin. Her breath came shallow and uneven.

Her willpower stretched thin, every instinct clashing with the call to surrender.

"Get out," she gasped, her voice cracking like old paint.

***

Izan didn't move. He let her push him away with words alone.

"You think I will harm you?" He asked, not with threat but with disbelief. "That I would betray you?" His brow creased. "I am made to serve the one who called. To protect. To pleasure. Forever. You marked me with your blood and ink, Sirati. With your internal fire. You summoned what you secretly crave."

It took her a breathless moment to realize she wasn't drowning in her own fear, but in his heat. The walls pulsed around her; the floor quivered beneath her feet. The air sharp in her lungs.

The room vibrated, as if it, too, was struggling under the pressure of this new reality. She had never known silence could be so loud. Each breath felt hotter, tighter, and the only thing with any control was Izan.

He stood in perfect stillness, radiating with an aura that could melt steel.

She braced herself against the corner, palms pressed to the paneling, fingers twitching with adrenaline. Each rapid inhale burned as if she were breathing in embers instead of air.

"Roxy," he said, his voice curled around her name like a promise.

It was a word, a plea, a claim. He was as real as the sweat beading on her skin.

"No," she breathed, disbelief and desperation shaping the denial. "I don't want—" But it was impossible to pretend she hadn't done what she'd done. Her mind was a riot of loneliness and fantasies crashing into this—this impossible man, this creature of fire and now flesh.

"I am not here to take. But we have a bond," Izan continued, each word like a coal tossed into the flame. "Not symbolic. Elemental. True as breath. You cannot ignore it, Ashling. Not without consequence."

Her breath caught.

Her head spun, a feverish reel she couldn't stop.

"Consequence?" she asked, voice strangled and thin. The word cracked something inside her.

He looked toward the windows, toward the street, toward the shimmering heat that anyone could see rising from the concrete of the city. "It's already begun."

"What's begun?" she asked, voice raw.

Izan's eyes bore into her, molten gold, eternal. "The fire you resist does not disappear. It spreads." He lifted a hand, palm up, showing her the ghost of flame that sparked there, vanishing before it could form. "Every time you resist, the heat seeks somewhere else to go. It is in the air. In the street. The pulse of this world feels it. Your denial is ignition."

Her throat worked. Sweat trailed down her temple.

"Christ," she gasped. Her knees trembled, threatening to give. Roxy's fingers clutched at her thigh, feeling the burn of the rune.

The reminder of his impossibility thrummed like a separate heartbeat, consuming her from the inside out.

He took a step closer, still a monument of control and heat, and the surrounding air shimmered. Her instincts shrieked for her to run, to flee, but she was trapped by the truth he brought with him.

"This is nuts. You're nuts," she insisted, desperation edging her voice. "I can't — this isn't real. You're not real."

"I am more real than your denial," he countered. "I am your longing, given form."

Roxy pressed her palm to the rune on her thigh, her fingers trembling.

"Feel it," Izan said, low and sure. "Your doubt does not make it less so. Every beat, every breath, every refusal to claim me strengthens it."

The room pulsed with his words, and the temperature seemed to climb by the second. As sweat beaded along her collarbone, she felt the tight, airless space close in around her. Even the tattoo guns and tools on nearby surfaces trembled, metal rattling like tiny bones, like the whole damn shop was shaking itself apart.

"If you don't want to hurt me, then why don't I feel safe?" she snapped, trying to regain a foothold of control in this insanity. She pressed her back flat against the corner once more, keeping her eyes on him.

Izan exhaled a breath that threatened to ignite. "Your mind thinks you want safety. Control. But your soul knows better."

The world swayed, danced in heated shadows. "What do you mean, my soul?" Roxy choked, and the panic tasted like iron. She could feel her resistance stretching thin.

He watched her, unfaltering, the certainty of ages in his voice. "It is not just your heart that calls me. Your will, your fire, all that you are and cannot hide. We are fated to be."

She shook her head, defiant and lost, and the air felt like molten glass against her skin. "And what, the city's just gonna burn because you say so?" She was stalling, falling, feeling the fight turn traitor in her blood.

"The fire is mine, Roxy. But it is also yours. This city is at the center of what we are. Of what we will be." He let the sentence hang between them.

A vow, a threat, a promise she wasn't ready to make.

***

The breath she took could have been her last—it tasted that raw, that dangerous. Roxy had one chance to save herself, and it stood inches from her, made of skin and smoke and everything she might want if she dared.

"Leave," she said, and the word scalded her throat as it escaped.

Was it terror or disbelief? She didn't know; she only knew she would burn alive if he didn't leave.

Izan stood, watching her unravel in a thousand ways at once. His eyes were a smolder, a waning fire. "Deny me if you must, but know this: the fire you lit does not burn in you alone."

Roxy flinched as though struck. It would have hurt less than the hope she caught flickering there, in the depths of molten gold that seared their final gaze into her memory.

"Get out," she forced again, but even as she said it, she felt the lie catch in her ribs. A raw, insistent denial tore through her.

Her heart screamed for what her voice wouldn't allow.

"As you wish," Izan accepted her command, and it felt like a brand tearing from her flesh. He closed his eyes, and she suddenly knew he did it so she wouldn't see how much her words hurt. "For now."

His body dissolved, losing shape and structure, turning gaseous and weightless. Ribbons of ash and tendrils of smoke curled from his skin, floating into the air and vanishing like a prayer burned to nothing.

For a moment, he was everything.

And then he was gone.

***

Roxy staggered, half-expecting the world to crash down around her. But the only thing that crashed was the sound of her pulse, wild and untethered. The shop felt even smaller without him, hotter, like she was the last thing left to consume.

The temperature rose in violent leaps, an unbearable force with nothing to contain it. The air sizzled and shimmered, dancing in waves like a taunt. Roxy was at the molten center, no longer protected by Izan's presence, but left to burn under the weight of it. She fumbled for the lights, flipping the switch with fingers too hot to feel.

Nothing.

Again, nothing. The fluorescents were dead, as if he'd taken even their glow with him. Her heart sank into a deep, terrifying place. The entire shop felt like it was collapsing inwards, like she would vanish into the thick and pulsing dark.

Roxy clawed for her phone, its surface slick with sweat and uncertainty. She needed light, a voice, a connection to something that wasn't Izan. Her thumb slipped, and she almost dropped it, fingers clumsy with the betrayal of panic.

She felt her legs give, sinking against the wall until she hit the floor, crumpled and drained. Her arms wrapped around herself, but they couldn't hold the pieces together.

Roxy had thought she was strong; strong enough to face down anything—but now?

She felt small.

Mortal.

On fire from the inside out.

The groan of metal was her only companion, loud and final, like it shared her agony. As her neighborhood lost power, the air conditioner went with a death rattle.

She was truly alone with her own undoing.

The rune on her thigh throbbed, merciless and raw. There was no relief from its pulse, no distance from the way it beat with more certainty than her heart. She hugged her knees, trying to hold on to herself in the sea of heat, and fear, and denial.

But even with Izan gone, the burn didn't stop.

It expanded, fierce and all-consuming, like a love letter written in flame.

Her breaths came hard and fast. It didn't make sense. She'd sent him away; shouldn't it be over? Shouldn't that make it stop? Her mind was a wasteland, stripped of the control she thought would save her.

Deny me if you must.

The words refused to die. They chased themselves around the walls of her skull, scorching everything in their path. The more she pushed against it, the more they branded her with their truth.

The fire you lit does not burn in you alone.

Roxy tried to smother the fear with her own voice, but she couldn't elude it, couldn't turn away from what she knew. She wasn't scared of the creature she had summoned, wasn't even scared of the city beyond these suffocating walls.

No, the most terrifying thing of all was the raw and reckless thing inside her—the thing that had called him, made him real, and then shattered when she told him to go.

She clenched her teeth, tasting salt, and desperation, and a desire she couldn't control. A desire she had spent a lifetime pretending didn't exist. The hunger was immense. So much bigger than she'd ever let it be.

She didn't need to look outside to know that Izan was right.

The city was feeling it now—the breathless heat, the churning want. Beyond the darkened windows, it was beginning to sweat, to warp, to pulse like her own private hell.

And in the center of the heat-storm was Roxy, small and crumpled, and losing control of everything except the knowledge that he would be back.

THE CITY MELTS

THE CITY AWOKE TO an inferno; each block and alley scorched in furious heat. In the area closest to *Veil and Ink*, a few patches on the asphalt of the road sweated and oozed like spent ink, and the occasional cries of car alarms broke against the heavy air as tires gave way, spilling their blackened guts into the street.

Roxy watched it all from her window, her skin glistening, the heat creeping into every pore and breath like a living, burning thing. The power had returned sometime in the middle of the early morning and inside, the shop was a tomb of suffocating warmth, and the constant thrum of ceiling fans and the occasional burst of hot wind sounded like the panicked flutter of trapped birds. She'd opened early, hoping the distraction might dull her restless mind, but even in the shade, she felt Izan's presence.

Her phone lit up with Raven's taunts.

> I'm gonna be late. Bus routes are running behind because some of the buses are broke down. News says it's from the heat. Who would have thunk it? In other news, Satan called, he wants his weather back.

Followed by:

Pretty sure we're all gonna melt. Use your
new Spellbook and conjure up cold brew or
a goddamn ice spell, boss!

Roxy almost dropped the phone, her laugh high, brittle, and sharp as the throbbing pulse of the rune on her thigh. If she only knew! At least she could always count on Raven to make her laugh.

The news anchor's voice, grim and theatrical, leaked from a television in the corner. "An unprecedented heatwave continues to grip the metro area," he declared, each word cracking like dry wood. "In addition to expecting more rolling brownouts, the city manager is reporting that bus routes are running behind schedule and emergency services are overwhelmed. Authorities urge residents to stay indoors and hydrate unless it's absolutely necessary to go outside."

Roxy rolled her eyes. *Like that would make a difference. This isn't natural.*

The rune's persistent throb reminded her it was only the beginning.

It had spread in the night while she slept naked, sprawled across her bed, a sheet twisted around one thigh, sweat plastering her hair to her neck. The delicate spiral of flame and thorns had bled across her hip in thorny new branches, blooming upward toward her ribs like something alive.

If it had been her own work, she would have been filled with pride; the rune, though terrifying, was exquisite.

In her bathroom earlier she had stared at it, silent, her fingers trembling as she reached down and traced it. But it still throbbed and was hot.

Her fingers skittered back as if she'd touched a stovetop.

But, it had convinced her like nothing else had last night, that Izan had been real.

"No," she'd whispered. "No, no, no."

She stumbled to the freezer, yanked open the drawer, and grabbed a handful of ice, cramming it into a kitchen towel; pressed it to the rune.

It melted almost instantly. Water soaked through the fabric, dripping to the floor. She dropped the wet cloth to the floor. Let it fall. Let the water steam from her skin. There was nothing else she could do.

Her eyes traced the streets again, a panorama of chaos. Across the way, a man in a Hawaiian shirt wrestled with a hose that had melted at the nozzle, spurting pitiful streams of water into the dense air. Dogs lay sprawled in the scant shadows, their tongues lolling, every inch of the world wilting beneath the relentless assault. She imagined she could taste the desperation, metallic, and biting, as though the City itself were a living beast, gasping and heaving. And at the center of its pain, she felt him. He was a pulse, a shadow, a presence that crept beneath her skin and settled like fire.

Inside, the air simmered with something more than heat, a tangible, electric heaviness that wrapped around her like an unwanted embrace. *Veil and Ink*, usually a refuge of creative chaos, now felt like a crucible, the boundaries of its walls closing in.

A dragon's mouth, she thought wryly, *and I'm the sacrifice.*

The sharp tang of ink mixed with the heat, the smell thick enough to choke. She wiped her forehead with the back of her hand, a trail of damp and frustration left behind. She was losing control, and she hated the taste of it, hated the way it caught in her throat and refused to let go. Even the soft flicker of fluorescents seemed accusing, buzzing like angry wasps. She flipped the lights off and slouched onto the shop's worn-out couch, hoping to clear her head, but everything pulsed with the same relentless beat, like blood, like desire.

Like Izan.

Her phone's sharp buzz made her jump, the sound slicing through the silence.

She fumbled for it, grateful for the distraction, already knowing who it would be. Raven, always quick with a quip, even in Hell's waiting room.

> You die in this freakish heatwave yet? Leave your vast empire to me. I'll totally avenge your ghost!

Roxy managed a smile, small and crackling, like dry leaves catching flame. "Asshole," she muttered, but it was fond, affection threading through the sarcasm. Typical Raven: wicked and precise, slicing right through to the core.

Raven had told her once that her mother was a psychic, but she didn't buy the mystical side of things. Called it woo-woo crap.

But Roxy suspected even Raven could sense something was off with her. She was smart like that.

> It's dead and I'm dying here. Need anything from beyond the grave?

She typed back with difficulty, realizing that if she didn't answer Raven would get worried. She didn't need her to get wrapped up in this.

Another quick reply came, quick as Raven's mouth.

> A damn snowstorm. Still want me to come in?

> Stay home and stay cool, sweetie.

> Thanks, boss. I hear that the damn buses are hotter than Satan's butthole!

She set the phone down; her chuckle escaping before it could take proper shape. The rune on her thigh shifted against the thin denim of her short-shorts, a gentle scrape of fabric that made her skin tingle and her stomach churn.

She had thought to make the tattoo hers, something she'd chosen to mark her skin and her life with. Now it felt like a brand, alive and unruly, a tether to things she'd barely comprehended.

It wasn't the first time she'd acted before thinking. A quick inventory of her life over the past few years would show the pattern: no family, few friends, fleeting lovers. It was always easier to leave than be left, easier to abandon than be abandoned.

But this, she realized, was different. This had a will of its own.

Izan also had a will of his own and she knew deep inside he was not easily shaken off. The thought itself was a brand, searing in its intimacy.

From the street, she heard more tires explode in staccato bursts, a grim music in the furnace of the City.

The phone rang, then eventually silenced as customers canceled appointments, unable to endure the heat. She scrawled "Hell Week" across the appointment book and sighed, the sound rattling against the charged air. Even if she had a walk-in, she wasn't sure she could work.

Determined to break free of her own thoughts, she sank into her workspace and picked up a sketchbook, her fingers already itching for distraction. The page seemed to shimmer under her touch, the lines she drew writhing like snakes, curling into themselves, jagged and unruly, a map of her mind and her guilt. The sketches mocked her, scorching in their intent, taunting with the knowledge she'd called this heat upon them all.

Again, the ceiling fan's dull whir became a taunt, a mocking reminder that nothing—not wind, not distance, not sarcasm—could cool what she'd unleashed. She snapped the sketchbook shut, the noise like a gunshot in the smothered silence. There was no escaping this. No cooling it down.

Roxy rested her head on the desk, letting the frantic pulse of her thoughts and the rune beat together. Maybe, just maybe, they'd sync up long enough to find a rhythm she could bear.

Outside, another tire screamed and died.

***

That night, sleep didn't come gently—it consumed her, curling around her like smoke through cracks, licking at the raw edges she'd tried to hide.

In the dream, he rose from the heat her body couldn't forget—no longer a man, nor yet a memory, but the echo of every desire she'd ever buried alive. His eyes burned like embers that knew her name. His skin glowed gold beneath ghostlight, radiant and wrong and hers. Every graze of his fingers felt like a solar flare — intimate, destructive, impossible to survive. His breath fanned over her skin in whispers, not of comfort, but of need — hers, his, indistinguishable.

Ashling, he called, voice molten, echoing through her like smoke curling into lungs not meant to breathe it. *Accept me. Be mine.*

She shattered under the sound of it. Her name on his tongue was a command and a prayer. Her resistance dissolved, fluttering into ash as his hands mapped the wild terrain of her body — greedy, reverent, unrelenting. The rune pulsed in her skin like a second heart, beating in rhythm with his mouth. Every kiss was a brand. Every touch, a claim.

Her dream-self arched against him, naked and hungry, need rising in her like a tide she no longer tried to turn. He worshipped her not with words, but with flame—his mouth carving devotion down her stomach, his weight pressing her into the sheets like she was something sacred, something to be marked and made holy. Her cries weren't fear — they were offerings.

She gave in. Gave up. Gave everything.

He was fire and god and gravity.

His skin against hers sparked like live wires—each graze a burst of heat, each slide a slow combustion. His fingers threaded through her hair, into her mind, curling around thoughts she hadn't even dared to feel. Even the space between them burned: heat wreathed her wrists, her thighs, the soft curve of her breast. Her nipples peaked against the steel of his chest, and when he groaned—deep, guttural, like she'd answered something ancient—it was all she could do not to beg.

The glowing patterns of the rune in her dream pulsed like a living vow, each line coiling tighter around her flesh, igniting desire into something more dangerous—devotion. The heat didn't just brand her.

It welcomed her.

Izan moved above her like fire given form—breath, body, need. His presence consumed the room, the air, the fragile shell of control she'd built around her heart. Every exhale scorched her skin, his hunger bleeding into her like smoke in silk, filling every space until there was no more room for doubt.

Sirati, he breathed against her throat, his voice ash and reverence. The syllables pressed into her skin like ritual. *Be mine.*

She already was.

His. Entirely. More than she had ever been her own.

Her body opened beneath him without thought, without fear. The last defenses melted beneath the weight of his touch. His mouth descended, brushing across her breasts with unbearable patience—slow, reverent, circling her nipples with heat and wetness until she arched, gasping, aching for more. Her moan fractured the silence.

Izan, she cried, voice thinned to air that didn't even feel like hers—it felt like him.

He growled in response, low and molten, a sound that rumbled through her bones and pooled between her thighs.

Her body betrayed every secret she'd tried to bury. She was coming apart at the seams—fear unraveling, caution erased. She was a canvas stretched taut beneath his hands, inked not with symbols but with sensation. Her body trembled as he carved his worship into her flesh with mouth, with tongue, with heat.

I'm yours, she gasped, the words catching like sparks in the space between them—not a confession, but a surrender. Her limbs wrapped around him, her back arched into the flames, and all that she had denied roared to life inside her. Her breath caught in time with his, tangled and hot, their bodies writing the only truth she had left: this was love set on fire, and she would never run from it again.

But even as her body arched into him, even as his hands made altars of her skin, a distant part of her—quiet, aching—knew this was only a dream. That it would vanish like breath against glass, and daylight would come to strip her bare, leaving behind only the ghost of his touch.

The emptiness would be waiting. That quiet, cruel shape she'd never named aloud.

And still—she gave herself to him.

To the fire. To the weight. To the ache that had waited a lifetime to be seen.

His hands roamed like scripture, mapping her body in reverent strokes, each one more devastating than the last. Heat rose between them, wild and blistering, threatening to brand her down to the bone. Her back bowed beneath it, caught in the sweet agony of a flame that wanted everything. As if the dream itself had teeth. As if it might finally consume the last corner of her that still knew how to say no.

She wanted that.

Feared it.

Thrilled at it.

Danger curled around the edges of her desire, dark and exciting as midnight—an endless tide she no longer had the strength to swim against.

Mine, he said again, a vow carved into heat, into air, into her.

Her skin burned where he touched her—not with pain, but with a love too bright to bear. The rune thrummed between them like a third heartbeat, echoing the pull in his gaze, the ache in his hands, the force of his longing.

His fingers slipped between her thighs with maddening precision. No hesitation, no doubt. The contact was devastating—direct, deliberate, and ruinous. She cried out, hips lifting to meet him, every muscle coiling, her breath catching as if her body could barely withstand the pressure.

He held her there—on the cusp, on the edge—his other hand pressed flat over the rune on her hip like he was keeping her tethered to the fire they had made.

The pleasure built like a storm behind her ribs, unbearable and infinite.

And still, she didn't beg.

She opened.

His mouth worshipped a path down her throat, over the notch of her collarbone, lower still. Each kiss a fiery brand. Each breath a flaming benediction. Down her stomach he moved, reverent, deliberate—like he was praying with his mouth and her body was the altar.

When he reached the space between her thighs, she opened for him without thought, without pride—only with hunger. Desperate. Reckless. Ready.

He breathed against her, heat and want rolling from his lips like a promise.

Her hips surged upward, seeking him, trembling for him.

She was unraveling—thread by thread, grip by grip, the careful stitching of her control coming undone in his hands.

She surrendered.

To him. To the fire. To the storm building beneath her skin.

Pleasure surged like a tide breaking the shore—violent, sacred, final. She came apart beneath him, hips jerking, hands fisting the sheets, mouth open in a wordless cry that only the dream would hear.

And just as she reached for something she couldn't name — something whole, something real —

— Roxy woke.

Gasping.

The dream clung to her like sweat, like smoke. Her skin gleamed under the faint light spilling through the window, every inch flushed and burning. The sheets were twisted ropes around her legs, holding her in the ghost of his arms.

Her heart thundered in her chest, wild and hollow and wanting.

She reached down, fingers brushing the rune. It pulsed. Alive!

***

The connection in the dream had been absolute. A completion she couldn't deny, couldn't escape. The heat of it filled the room, pressing in like a living thing. The sheets clung to her skin, wet and transparent, outlining the hard lines of her nipples, the sharp rise and fall of her chest.

She sat up, breathless, dizzy, burning, her hair falling around her like a halo of dark, damp strands. Her bedroom was stifling, thick with a presence she could almost touch. Could almost taste. Her pulse refused to calm, racing, relentless, as though her heart hadn't left the dream at all.

"Izan," she whispered into the darkness, his name both an ache and a balm. It hung in the room, more than a memory, more than a ghost. The rune thrummed hot and vivid, creeping further, wild as his need.

Wild as her own.

He was there, impossibly there, a silhouette of raw need at the foot of her bed.

Izan.

Real. Solid. Watching her.

His golden eyes glowed with an inner fire, his skin lit from within by a constellation of embers. He was all elements and intensity, a creature of flesh and longing that eclipsed her senses.

Roxy didn't speak. Couldn't. Her breath caught as he crossed to the side of the bed closest to her. The air bent around him. She felt his heat before he touched her — fingertips hovering just above her skin.

It should have terrified her. The weight of him in this world, the reality of his presence. But terror came second, far behind the rush of uncontained want that ripped through her, shaking every part of her into helpless, thrilling awareness. Her heart stuttered and leaped, her skin alight with the promise of his touch.

"Izan," she started, her voice a cracked and breathless thing. But she couldn't continue, couldn't find the words or the will to speak them. The force of his desire left her raw, exposed, every inch of her pleading for him with traitorous insistence.

"Your body called to me," he said, voice like smoke and honey, with a thousand shades of belonging. The weight of it pressed against her chest, wrapped around her wrists. "And I came."

Her lips parted. She should say no. She should tell him to leave. She didn't.

Her body leaned toward him, defying the fractured restraints of her mind.

She wanted him.

Oh God, she wanted him with a force that shattered.

She reached for him.

He cupped her face.

The kiss was a blaze, a smoldering brand that seared her very bones in a furnace of worship.

He devoured her with heat and hunger, lips bruising, tongue insistent. The sheet slipped from one shoulder. His hand grazed the edge of her breast.

His mouth was the answer to every fear, every want, every defense.

Roxy let herself fall. Fall into the heat, and weight, and promise of him, each second an eternity of burning. She gave in to it; to him. Her fingers tangled in his smoke-black strands of hair, pulling him ever closer. Her body arched into his, needing to close the last impossible gap, needing to feel him with every atom of her skin, her being, her heart.

She kissed him back with a hunger that broke over her like Greek Fire on water, uncontained, all-consuming. It was everything she'd denied herself, denied them, and for that one heartbeat, for that one glorious, incandescent second, she let it be real. She let it fill her, claim her, burn her clean, and bright, and whole.

But terror was a vicious thing, an old familiar, and it lashed through her in an arc of desperation. It speared her with terrifying precision, lashing out before her heart could stop it, before her mind could rein it in.

She pushed away, gasping for air, for distance, for the control she knew was already lost.

Her fingers shoved at his chest, desperate and confused. Terrified.

Roxy's lips moved, searching for the distance she should want, the safety she should demand. But her heart raced past logic, past fear, and all that came was a gasp of broken denial. "I can't…"

It was a lie, and they both knew it. She couldn't keep this away, couldn't keep him away, no matter how desperately she pretended otherwise.

She looked into his eyes, wide and gold, filled with a sadness so deep it tore through her, deeper than the fire, deeper than the rune. Deeper than the doubt she'd carved herself with. Her world tilted, and for one impossible moment, Roxy was sure she'd finally, finally break.

***

"Roxy," he said, her name a choked whisper. The agony in his voice matched the tearing inside her, and she hated it.

Hated the way she'd given him hope, only to shatter it with her cowardice.

Izan stepped back. Not angry. Not hurt.

Only…

Broken.

"I would burn a thousand times to feel you beneath me but once," he rasped, each word a wound, each word a vow.

Then he vanished—ash and smoke unraveling into the heat.

And she was alone, more alone than she'd ever been. The taste of him lingered on her tongue, a bittersweet ghost of what could have been, what should have been, if she hadn't been so afraid to trust, to fall, to give in to the desire of both body and mind.

The scent of burning hung in the air, a testament to their shared and smoldering desire.

The room felt impossibly large, impossibly empty. It echoed with the loss of him, the loss of everything she couldn't bear to hold.

In the void between breaths, she thought she heard him whisper, "Sirati."

Sacred, reverent, hers.

She pressed her fingers to her lips, still swollen with the memory of his kiss, still tingling with the heat of him. It wasn't enough. Not even close.

Outside, a transformer exploded, a violent protest against the silence. The windows flashed with a shower of sparks, and she saw the City plunge into darkness, one block at a time.

The heat swelled, monstrous and alive, the entire world mirroring the chaos in her chest.

Her rejection made manifest.

FLAMES AND FRACTURES

HEAT FRACTURED THE STREETS like glass. The sun—bloated, unrelenting—clung to the sky like a curse, refusing to die.

Madness lit the city in flickering strobes of emergency, fractured red and blue lights stabbing through *Veil and Ink's* front window. Roxy leaned against the glass, her bare arms slick with sweat, watching the world unravel. A water main exploded, geysering through concrete like a wound torn open and over the surrounding panicked figures as vehicles raced past. Even from a block away, she could see it arc skyward, steam pouring off in billows. Across the street, power lines sagged like melting taffy, buzzing with fatigue.

The sirens screamed under the TV's panicked drone—power outages, fires, a world breaking apart.

Her phone buzzed with Raven's text.

Where the hell are you, boss?!

She stared at the message, thumb frozen above the screen hovering over the digital keyboard. But the weight of shame was heavier than her fingers. Her reflection caught her like a terrible secret, sweat-slicked and rippling beneath fluorescent lights that flickered and groaned like dying beasts.

Outside, asphalt bubbled, and the crowd scattered, dodging the chaos in silhouettes. She wiped a streak of moisture from the window with the edge of her glove, knowing the moment she did, it would return. Another distant explosion rumbled the shop and set off a spray of frantic car alarms, the noise as relentless as the heat. Her skin prickled under her tank top, the shirt glued to her like an accusation as she glared at the still-buzzing phone. Raven's words glowed on the screen, echoing louder in her head:

> Hello? Where the hell are you? Are you okay?

The shop's window air conditioner sputtered against the high temperatures, coughing into silence as lights pulsed a dim orange, staining the walls.

Roxy slapped the phone down on the counter and felt it hum beneath her palm, persistent as a mosquito bite. Her pulse quickened, the sensation trailing her nerves until it nested under her ribs and curled around her lungs. It was happening again. The rune pulsed beneath her tank top, the tendrils of ink having spread over her hip, curling up along her ribs like thorned vines.

It ached with every heartbeat, every refusal; like a firebrand carved into her flesh.

She pulled her burgundy-streaked, shoulder-length brown hair back from her neck, exhaling like she could force the heat from her body if she tried hard enough. Ink stains darkened the edges of her gloves, smudged lines bleeding up her bare arms, turning her skin to an abstract of self-inflicted scars. She turned away from the counter, her legs stiff beneath her, and headed toward the back of the shop, gathering scattered magazines and taking inventory of ink cartridges as her mind raced.

Sweat pooled between her shoulder blades, sticky and metallic-smelling, and her tank top clung worse with every step. The fluorescents crackled and buzzed above her, throwing her shadow long and warped against the walls. The metal piercings at her ears and nose itched and glowed with trapped heat, until she thought they'd leave permanent marks, causing her to remove them. As she moved farther from the window, her breath caught like a hook under her chest, the air turning as thin and unreliable as her own will.

The back room offered little relief. The air hung thick as molten iron; the walls crowded with uneven shelves, scattered drawings, spare needles, and ink supplies. Roxy slammed the door and leaned against it. The desperation to get out from under Raven's text vibrated in her bones, her own name beating against her skull in time with her pulse.

How could she tell her she was responsible for all of this? That she had called forth some fire genie from a bottle, and unless she surrendered herself to him, they were all gonna fry?

Raven would think she was crazy, or at the very least that her brain was affected by the heat.

The mini-fridge in the back room shuddered, expiring. She yanked it open, grabbed a tray of ice meant for compresses, and pressed a handful to her face.

It dissolved, trickling through her fingers like an accusation.

Water streamed down her chin, soaking the front of her shirt. Her palm was empty before she could even try to drink.

"Fuck," she muttered, sliding down to sit with her back against the wall. The tiled wall was too warm.

Everything was.

The room dimmed as the last flickers of fluorescent light strangled out under another brownout. She opened the door, which left her under the uneven glow of the scorching, sun-drenched streets. Her phone buzzed again and again from the front counter, distant but insistent. Roxy laid down and rested her forehead against the cement floor, as if she could absorb its chill through sheer force of will.

Her voice cracked with the effort of a whispered confession, "I did this. I let this happen."

She moved to grab her phone from the counter just as it buzzed again. She sat down on the floor next to the counter and read the text.

Roxy, are you okay? Seriously, don't ghost me now! This heat is wrong. Everyone's freaking out.

Roxy opened the keyboard. Typed one word.

Sorry.

She erased it before she could send it.

Instead, she buried her face in her knees.

The shop's stale air thickened with sulfur and sweat, stinging her eyes and scraping her throat with each breath. She rolled onto her back, ink-stained fingers spreading uselessly over the aching rune on her side. The tattoo pulsed beneath her tank top, the lines twisting and tightening across her body. She curled into herself, nails digging into skin as she wrestled with the words she couldn't bring herself to say. A part of her wished it would take her down with it — heatwave, power outage, burning sky and all.

But it wasn't only that. And she couldn't admit it, even if she was brave enough to try. She stared up at the ceiling, metal tools shimmering with heat on the nearby trays, Raven's abandoned sketches curling at the edges. Sirens howled past the shop, their panic-stricken urgency drowning out the useless, slowing ceiling fans.

***

Night crawled in like a thief through a shattered window—it *bled*, slow and smoky, through the cracks of a dark city trying not to scream.

Without the lights, the tattoo shop steeped in a bruised kind of sepia—washed in the low, molten glow bleeding through the windows from a sky still on fire. Ash drifted in slow, ghostlike spirals down the glass, fine and gray as powdered bone. Sirens wailed, distant and desperate, then died into silence. The city didn't rest. It held its breath like something cornered—waiting for night to save it, or swallow it whole.

As the shadows deepened, Roxy watched the rune swell with light. She blinked in surprise. And then she saw him.

"Izan," she whispered.

Izan materialized at the threshold of the shop, his broad frame silhouetted by the distant fires.

He looked unlike the first night she saw him. Now he was unsteady, and nearly human; his molten bronze skin dulled to a weathered copper, as if his inner flame had cooled, and his shoulders hunched forward in exhaustion or defeat. He no longer had that hungry aura of a summoned god. He moved like someone who had lost something.

Roxy pressed herself against the wall as he moved a step closer, his gold-glowing eyes fixed on her like a desperate plea.

"I felt you again," he said, his voice roughened by something more than smoke.

She straightened against the side of the counter, every muscle wired tight. "Stay there."

He did.

His eyes didn't burn—they shimmered. Their gold dulled to ember.

"What do you want me from me?" She whispered.

"I want to claim your love, and I want you to claim mine. In essence, I want your soul, Sirati."

"You said that you wouldn't hurt me." Her whisper was laced with terror.

"I only want to love you. But I will not steal what must be freely given." Izan's voice dropped to a rough whisper, edged with grief and certainty. "I came to show you this."

He was wearing a loose fitting red Moroccan gandura over white linen sirwal pants. He raised one arm and pulled the fabric from his shoulder. There, across his chest and collarbone, a matching rune had formed — thorned, sprawling, alive.

Roxy's heartbeat thundered, amplifying the heat that threatened to swallow her whole. The thin fabric of her shirt clung to her skin, soaked in fear, her breath erratic and wild. She met his gaze, defiant, but stunned. She pressed her palm against her own skin, felt her rune pulse back.

He gestured to her rune, now vivid beneath her tank top, and moved back from her, letting the silence hang between them like a weight.

"What ... what does that mean?" She finally asked.

"Our souls entwine, my spark," he said. "Despite your refusal. No matter how far you push, the call lives in both of us now. You etched me into this world, and it has changed us both."

The air shimmered between them. Not hot—intimate. Like something sacred was trying to speak.

"You think this was about me," he continued, softer now. "But it never was. It's about you. Your refusal to be seen. To be wanted. To burn."

Her mouth opened. Closed. Her body trembled. Her skin flushed with heat that wasn't from the room.

Roxy closed her eyes against the sharp tug beneath her ribs, the call of something far deeper than her body. It hurt more than she expected, like she was already burning from the inside out. Her body ached. Not just with want, but with the echo of his truth. "I told you I don't want this!"

Izan shook his head, his eyes reflecting the city's inferno. His smoke-black hair lay against his skin, catching in the thick, stifling air. The heat shimmered between them, absent of his earlier predatory intensity, now a muted flicker of resignation.

"It is beyond want," he said. "It is who we are. The choice has always been yours. But, my Sirati, I would willingly suffer the raging flames and winds of Jahannam to feel you beneath me for eternity," Izan said. The way he looked at her then—like she was the one vanishing—split her down the middle.

Tears blurred Roxy's vision as a savage heat clawed through her, something far more consuming than temperature. Her body ached with a want she couldn't bring herself to name. She pulled tighter into herself, raw and exposed, her skin flushed for reasons she wouldn't admit even now.

"Take it back!" Her voice cracked and broke as terror choked its way up her throat. "Whatever you did to me, take it back!" She sobbed. "Please."

Izan held his ground, sorrow and longing carving lines across his once-sure features. He made no move toward her, the patience in his stance her undoing.

He bowed his head, that simple act weighted with ancient sorrow. "I have great power and can do many things, but I cannot unmake the fire inside you. Only you can decide whether to feed it or let it consume all."

"I can't—" Her breath hitched as her soul clawed at its cage, and the words twisted from her mouth like a wounded thing.

He didn't vanish all at once. He faded like a memory—first his edges, then his shape, then the last flare of his gaze.

And then he was gone; dissolved into smoke and ash.

The silence screamed.

The windows cracked under the pressure of heat. The sound of distant gunshots rang out next, as the criminal element took advantage of the collapse of the city to create more havoc and mischief. The night sky outside the shop glowed a blistering orange, the color of combustion.

Ash fell like snow, cloaking the street in front of the shop with death's soft exhale—gentle, gray, and final.

Roxy collapsed. To the truth. To the ache that wouldn't leave her.

She stayed there, hunched and silent, pressing her ink-stained hands against the floor as if she could stop the world from fracturing.

And in the furnace of that moment, she finally believed —

The world was burning.

And it was her fault.

SURRENDER TO THE FIRE

THE CITY BURNED LIKE it wanted to erase itself from history.

Ash drifted through the air like snow, settling over broken glass and blistered pavement in a fine gray hush. The skyline bled orange, jagged silhouettes piercing a sky gone bruise-black with smoke. Sirens wailed—then choked into silence, smothered by heat too thick for sound to breathe. Windows cracked. Pavement split. Somewhere, tires burst like overfilled balloons.

She was the match and the tinder. And to someone else, that kind of power might have been magnificent.

But Roxy's world had spiraled into ruin. The fire inside her burned hotter than the ones around her, and there was no salvation in distance—only exposure.

She had thought shutting down meant staying safe. That keeping her heart behind glass would protect it.

Instead, it made her brittle.

Hollow.

Open to ghosts. Closed to everyone who ever mattered.

The ache of Izan's absence split her open, left her raw and desperate. Her pulse roared through her veins, vibrating in her bones. Her fingers dug into her palms.

She finally admitted it.

She wanted him. She wanted him more than her own breath.

It was wild. It was crazy. She didn't even know him, but she was drawn to him like a moth to flame; like he was the other half of her.

The realization consumed her: she didn't want to be alone anymore.

Roxy had built walls around herself, only to watch them collapse. She'd thought pushing love away would protect her. She was wrong. She didn't feel strong. She didn't feel safe. She felt weak and exposed as the rest of the burning world, her own defenses a trap that starved her while the city burned, bled, and warped. The heat curled inside her like a living thing. Panic threatened at the thought of going to him, but a need deeper than fear made her determined to find him. Her heart howled and twisted with urgency. Her throat choked on heat and truth.

She needed to stop what was happening; to the city and to herself. And she needed him.

Her thighs, her ribs, her thoughts: everything that the rune touched pulsed with reckless need. She rose from the ground with a new purpose. Determination, pure and bright, pushed her up and over her fears. If he was a creature of fire, then she was its equal. She'd denied herself for too long. Denied them both. The room for resistance had collapsed inwards, just like the city around her. Just like her heart. The only way out was through him, through the blaze of their longing.

The burn wouldn't stop, couldn't stop, until she found him again.

Izan. Her mind ached with his name.

She ran out of the shop, pulled by a magic she didn't understand, only knowing that she had to find him.

Her shoes stuck to the softening asphalt. The heat rolled over her skin in relentless waves, thick as oil, heavy as guilt. The rune on her thigh had spread like wildfire up her side, curling in thorned spirals over her hip and ribs. It pulsed now, a living brand, syncing to the frantic rhythm of her heartbeat.

She no longer blamed the weather. Or the city. Or the broken grid. The truth blistered across every inch of her skin: she had done this. Her fear. Her refusal. Her hunger.

Each breath scalded her throat. Each step felt like penance. And somewhere through the smoke-veiled chaos, her soul screamed in one direction only.

Izan.

Sweat was a distant memory, evaporating before it formed. Her shorts clung to her like a second skin, a second life. Her hair tangled and whipped behind her as she pushed forward, faster than she thought possible.

She wanted this. Wanted him. The desperate pulse of her heart told her what her mind refused to admit: she didn't care if it destroyed her.

The only thing worse than burning was freezing. Freezing due to fear of a future that might never come to pass.

"I don't want to be alone anymore," she gasped, the words burning like a confession, like a prayer.

The rune glowed hot against her skin, searing and alive.

Every inch of her was fire and determination.

Her chest blazed with certainty. The heat no longer felt suffocating; it felt true. Her limbs moved with renewed purpose, her feet pounding against the cracked pavement, a frantic counterpoint to the pulse that drove her forward. She wouldn't run away. Not this time. The realization ripped through her like a storm, clearing away all hesitation, all fear.

It left nothing but raw need and clarity.

Her thoughts clanged as loud and furious as the fire bells in the distance.

Izan. She could almost see him now, golden, perfect, waiting for her. She was his, and he was hers. Her mind raced toward him, toward where she could feel him, pulling her body behind it like a comet's tail.

The air cracked with dry, static heat. Voices rose like a discordant choir: full of anger and confusion, fear and chaos. But her own voice was louder in her mind, loud as sirens, loud as truth.

It would never stop, never cool, until she reached him.

Until she reached for him.

Izan.

***

She found him not in the heavens or fire, but crouched behind her shop—an alley now shrouded in ruin and dumpster fires. His figure was dimmer than memory, bronze skin tarnished to copper, golden eyes barely flickering.

He was disappearing.

His form shimmered like a heat mirage, edges dissolving into vapor. Kneeling on cracked cement within a hastily drawn rune circle, he whispered words she couldn't hear, but felt deep in her marrow.

A ritual. A surrender. A goodbye.

"No," she rasped.

He didn't turn.

A rooftop on the other side of the alley groaned under the strain of heat. Chunks of scorched brick crumbled and fell. Still, he didn't move.

"Izan!"

His shoulders flinched at her voice.

She stumbled forward, legs trembling. Her skin seared with every step, sweat evaporating as fast as it formed. The rune on her side pulsed furiously, golden fire threading across her skin like veins lit from within.

He looked up.

And in his beautiful golden eyes, she saw it: the agony of a creature ready to die if it meant he wouldn't destroy what he loved.

He would take oblivion over her refusal, and it shattered her more than his presence ever had. Izan kneeled alone, the fires of the world dim compared to the despair in his eyes. He would leave, ready to sacrifice himself rather than risk Roxy's world.

She saw the shadows of grief etching his face and it shook her more than the crumbling city. The intensity of his departure was greater than anything she'd ever felt.

Izan's form flickered, smoke and sorrow lifting into the air like dust.

His voice came to her, a wound and a promise.

"I will not take what you will not give," he said. "Better to vanish back into the void than turn your world to ash."

The words cracked through her like a fault line.

The city writhed around him, smoke, fire, chaos — all paled beside the heartache in his gold-ember eyes.

This was her fault. His sadness, his isolation; all of it was because she had called him, bound him to her soul and then pushed him away, because she was too afraid to be claimed. Too afraid to accept what the universe had sent her. She felt the collapse in her own chest as he bowed his head. Nothing in the city burned hotter than her heart.

His presence drew her forward, the distance too far and too close at once.

Izan shimmered in the haze, beautiful and unbearable.

Her feet carried her to him, each step vibrating through the cracked pavement and the soles of her shoes. The pulse in her chest grew wilder with every breath. Her soul ached in time with the rune, ached with want, with panic, with recognition.

Izan was both infinite and fragile; both certain and defeated.

He wasn't leaving because he wanted to — he was leaving because she was too much of a coward to ask him to stay. Izan kneeled, hands on his knees. Accepting. Resigned. He closed his eyes to the world and waited for it to release him.

Tears of heat stung her eyes. Her selfish fear was their undoing. It had blinded her to the truth: it only hurt them both, only starved them until they couldn't survive. His devotion shattered her, left her heart cut and bleeding and on fire. She was killing him by pretending not to care. Killing them both.

His presence was consuming, but his absence — his absence would destroy her.

His form blurred at the edges, fragile and shimmering. Particles of his being lifted like ash into the super-heated air.

She wouldn't let it happen.

Roxy kneeled in front of him, breath hitching, and placed her palm over his heart. It was hot — not painful, not cruel, but alive.

Not human. But, His.

Her rune flared, and his chest glowed beneath her touch, matching the spirals etched across her own flesh.

Izan's eyes met hers, golden, sad, waiting for the one thing she had never given. Acceptance.

"I don't want to be alone anymore," she said, voice shaking but true.

The air shattered.

The bond between them broke open like a dam, power surging in waves that made the ground shudder. Izan surged up with a growl — low, guttural, not quite human. His arms wrapped around her, lifting her, his mouth crashing into hers.

It was not conquest.

It was collapse.

***

The distance that had felt eternal now was nonexistent. Her thoughts collided with her body, leaving no space for doubt. Nothing but need, need, and more need. The world spun. She wasn't afraid of him, but of how much she wanted him, how much she needed this to be true. She needed it like air.

Her chest ached with the weight of her decision.

It was the ache of something longed for, the ache of finally being whole.

It was unbearable. It was wonderful. It was inevitable.

Izan's eyes, wide and molten, told her everything she needed to know.

She reached for him with shaking hands, letting go of everything she'd used to hold herself back. Letting go of her anger, her skepticism, her cowardice. Her barriers and her bravado had no place here.

All she had to give him was herself, raw and willing, exposed and wanting.

But that is all he'd ever asked for. Her. All he'd ever wanted. His Sirati.

The contact shook the universe, shifted into something massive and wild. The rune flared gold beneath her fingers, beneath his skin. She felt the thrum of his heartbeat, the heat of him, the intensity she'd craved from the start. It was more than heat, more than desire.

It was fusion, and it was alive. Alive like she was alive, like they were alive, together and true. The air thickened around them, vibrating with magic.

Her breath caught in her throat, filled with Izan's essence, filled with awe and hope and light.

She didn't have to say it. He felt it. Her every wordless thought. Her every unspoken want.

His eyes blazed as her touch solidified him.

The connection grew wild, intense, beyond anything she'd ever known. The rune burst into golden flame, spreading in mirrored spirals over their bodies, over their world, binding them like living chains. Roxy moaned, her voice pure surrender, pure need.

Raw energy surged, flooding her senses, turning them into more than flesh and skin and bone.

It turned them into forever.

***

Izan's growl was an element, a breath, an atom. He seized her, fusing body to body, turning their world molten. His mouth claimed hers, worshipful, desperate, swaying with the force of his need. He wrapped her in his arms, unbreakable, and she was weightless as he carried her into a whirlwind of fire.

The universe shifted and folded around them and they landed on her bed.

Clothing burned away without flame, leaving nothing between their skin, their breath, their endless, beautiful surrender. Her tank top disintegrated beneath his hands. Her shorts floated away in ash. He laid her back against the sheets, hands trembling with reverence and hunger as he studied every inch of her bared skin. Skin on skin, their connection was a living, breathing thing.

"So beautiful," he whispered, his voice cracked open with awe. He pinned her to the mattress, the weight of him more than physical.

The rune blazed on their skin.

Golden fire bloomed over their bodies, vivid and consuming. The ink turned alive, as alive as their hearts; as alive as the desire that built between them.

Her fingers tangled in his dark smoke-haloed hair. Her hips arched up to meet his body. He slid against her with devastating slowness, kissing her throat, the softness of her breast, the curve of her ribs.

Every touch was a vow. Every gasp a confession.

The rune traced itself across them both, blooming in mirrored patterns from her thigh to his chest, curling in golden tendrils down his back and over her breasts. The marks pulsed with their joined heartbeat.

His mouth found her nipple and drew it in with aching tenderness, the heat of his breath turning her whimper into a plea. His hands roamed — over ribs, over hips, between thighs slick with desire.

Izan worshipped her with each touch, each kiss, every movement filled with raw and urgent need.

She arched into him, every barrier collapsing, every instinct screaming for more, for everything.

She clutched his shoulders, nails raking over the firelight in his skin.

"Izan," she breathed, lost to it, to him.

His arms wrapped around her, his strength uncontainable. The world spun, and they spun with it, a fevered blur of longing.

"Mine," he said, fierce and reverent.

"Yours," she gasped, and the word set them alight.

He entered her and a sound like thunder echoed through the air.

Her body opened to him like it had always waited just for him. The friction sparked across every nerve ending, the stretch exquisite and unbearable.

He thrust, slow and deep, and she cried out as the rune on her side exploded with gold.

They moved together in a rhythm older than memory, primal and sacred.

Her legs wrapped around him.

His hands slid beneath her, pulling her tighter to him as he pushed deeper.

The bedsprings cried out beneath them, wild and helpless, as their bodies melded together, into fire and flesh, into soul and spirit.

Heat coiled in her spine. The world narrowed to breathy gasps and sweat, and the sound of his name escaped from her throat again and again.

"I see you, Sirati," he said. "Every piece of your soul. Every flame you've tried to bury. I see all of you, and you are beautiful."

Roxy shivered at the edge of control, then past it, then into the beautiful unknown of them. His skin was bronze and perfect above her. Her voice was breathless, and it carried them higher, further, beyond where she'd ever let herself go. Her hands gripped his shoulders, pulling him closer, pulling him in with desperate insistence. He responded with a deep, molten sound that was more than a groan, more than a growl.

The raw power of their bond filled every inch of the room, every inch of their bodies, every inch of the world outside.

The universe bent. The world gave way.

It was pure want, pure claiming.

The pressure broke.

She came with a sob, blinding and shuddering, her back arching as gold fire flared from her skin.

He followed with a hoarse cry, his body shaking as he spilled into her, the rune sealing across their bodies like molten metal cooling into permanence.

He held her as if she was the only thing he could never bear to lose.

Her pulse crashed in her chest, dizzy, wild, free.

The city felt the shift as their union exploded into light.

The heat broke, sudden and impossible. A crack in the universe. A gasp of thunder.

And rain fell for the first time in days.

Fat drops hissed against glass and rooftop, turning smoke to steam. The city exhaled, steam rising from scorched streets like a benediction.

But Roxy only felt him.

Izan cradled her like something holy, his lips pressed to her temple.

He was hers, and she was his.

She looked at him, at his beautiful, devoted face, and felt the weight of forever press them close, press them into one being. The rune sang across their skin. Her soul sang with it.

"Mine," she said, and the world glowed.

"Always," he answered.

Her breath hitched, and for the first time in her life, she felt whole.

Alive!

Loved.

The fire no longer consumed her.

It had become her.

***

The dark clouds poured down, claiming every street and rooftop, cooling every inch of the furnace she'd created. The wind lifted, scattering the ash that covered the streets.

And through it all, Izan held her, kept her close, and with him she knew she was more than she'd ever been.

The city gleamed under the rain, cleansed, and she gleamed with it, her heart finally, truly alive.

Outside the window, steam rose from every inch of asphalt, ghosting into the cooling night. They stayed tangled together, limbs entwined, feeling the new pulse of the city.

Of them.

Of everything.

WHAT SURVIVES THE FLAME

RAIN FELL IN VIOLENT sheets, drumming the scorched streets in a percussive rage, filling gutters with frantic rivers. The inferno was over. Cracks spread like veins through the pavement outside *Veil and Ink*, but the fires had died, and the air no longer clawed at the lungs. A breeze stirred the humid air, heavy with wet ash and relief.

Roxy lay curled against Izan, skin to skin, their limbs tangled like new constellations. Heat and certainty rose from them in tender steam, soft against the battering storm. Her pulse matched the rhythm of his heart, of the rain, of the shared and living mark that bloomed across their bodies.

Her breath caught in her throat, a bittersweet tangle of relief and wonder. She'd been afraid to want, afraid to believe. Afraid that if she did, she would end up abandoned in the dark with nothing but her own foolish dreams.

But he was still here.

She was still here.

They were here, together.

Izan slept with the peaceful weight of one who had lived a thousand lifetimes and found his way home. His smoke-black hair clung to his temples in soft tendrils, damp with effort and intimacy. His bronze skin gleamed with sweat, his breath warm against her shoulder.

Roxy watched Izan, feeling a rush of tenderness as she traced the sharp angles of his jaw and the curve of his full mouth. Her fingertips skimmed the lines of his collarbone, tracing the places where ash and heat had marked him with their shared devotion. The runes twined across his chest, mirroring the ones that etched her own skin, mirroring the shape of her heart as it curled around his.

She watched the rise and fall of his chest, the perfect, unhurried pace of his breath. Even asleep, he held her, his arms a living promise that she would never be left behind. The weight of him was everything she hadn't allowed herself to wish for — intimacy without distance, love without condition.

"I love you," she whispered, the words more real than anything she'd ever spoken.

For the first time, her thoughts were still. They exhaled, soft as steam, weightless as rain.

Outside, the city groaned under the downpour, each raindrop a miniature reckoning as it kissed scorched concrete. The rooftops and streets shivered and spat, cooling in violent fits of steam like a fever broken.

But inside, Roxy felt only heat and connection, the steady pulse of her own soul connected to another. She closed her eyes and let the moment wash over her, let the sound of the storm fill her until there was nothing left to hold but him.

His presence was everything she had imagined and nothing she could have dreamed. Where once she would have fled, she now lingered. Where once she feared being caught, now she clung to him with a desperation made sweet by the certainty that he would never let go.

Her fingers traced the path of his skin, the living flame of the rune that linked them in a loop of burning devotion. His limbs tightened around her with the gravity of the universe, a beautiful weight she never wanted to lose.

She exhaled, the sound a soft and quiet surrender, and buried her face in the crook of his neck. Izan murmured in his sleep; a low and elemental sound. It made her heart stutter and leap, made the rune thrum like an open vein. He was everything she'd ever wanted — devotion, fire, someone so real they couldn't be ignored.

This is what it feels like, she thought, *to be alive in someone else's heart, to burn without fear of being abandoned.*

Her lips curved into a soft, breathless smile.

***

The tattoo shop had been trashed in the chaos. Walls damaged by the heat displayed bubbled paint and buckled paneling and drywall; shelving appeared to be scorched and warped; the pleather covered furniture was stiff, cracked and discolored, and the smell of smoke and scorched carpet rose like ghosts of what once was.

Roxy stood by the cracked front window in nothing but one of Izan's long shirts, watching the world breathe again. She held a chipped mug in her hands, the bitter, instant coffee long gone cold. She glanced behind her briefly at the shop. The destruction was vast, but it mirrored the landscape of Roxy's heart before Izan returned, before she allowed herself to want him without restraint.

She should have cared. But she didn't.

There was no grief. Just clarity.

She'd held on so tight to fear, to distance, to her stubborn independence, to the insistence of avoiding all risks of heartbreak. Held on until she almost let him slip away.

Once, she would have let the damage to her shop pull her under, and used it as an excuse to push him away, used it to say: this is the destruction that desire inflicts.

But now?

Now she held on tight to him, knowing that in the end, together, they could put all to rights. After all, these were just things and things could be repaired or replaced.

What truly mattered was what she had found in both herself and Izan: a connection that would last forever.

Footsteps splashed through the puddled sidewalk outside. A moment later, the front door creaked open.

Dripping wet, and soaked to the bone, Raven stood in the doorway in a drenched band tee and rain-slick jeans, eyes wide as they scanned the damage to the shop.

Her jaw slackened. She whistled low. "Holy hell, Roxy. Did a fire demon move in, or did you just get freaky with a flamethrower? Oh, no!" she exclaimed, heading into the back and looking at the melted coffee maker. "It's just toast! We can't live without coffee!"

Roxy turned toward her, hair damp and tangled, eyes darker than they'd ever been. And softer.

"I'll get you a new one," she smiled, then was interrupted by Izan's voice coming from up the stairs.

"Sirati, I will be down shortly to help you clean. Have you seen my shirt?"

Raven arched an eyebrow. Her gaze drifted upward to the ceiling, where smoke-stained ceiling tiles dwelled. She sniffed, nodded to herself, and looked at Roxy in surprise, seeing her outfit for the first time.

"Uh, huh? Just text me when you're human again. I'm going to the bodega. I will bring you back some real coffee."

She was gone in a rustle of wet footsteps.

***

Later that night, the world had collapsed into silence. Not the silence of abandonment, but the kind that follows a catastrophe — holy and hushed; full of aftermath and gratitude for being alive.

Roxy lay on her side in the nest of their shared bed, pressed against Izan's molten skin. His bronze flesh gleamed with the kiss of lingering heat, his black-scorched hair curling damp at his temples. One muscular arm draped over her waist, holding her with the certainty of someone who had once been ash and had now been named.

She traced slow spirals over his chest where the rune lived now — no longer a wound, no longer a curse. It pulsed faintly under her fingertips, warm and alive.

Rain tapped at the cracked windows, a steady rhythm like a heartbeat echoing from the sky.

"I told you I'd end up getting her a new machine," she murmured, but the joke died before it left her mouth fully formed.

Izan's golden eyes opened, soft and flame-bright in the low light. He said nothing at first. He only looked at her, watched her like she was his miracle.

Roxy leaned closer, pressing her palm flat against his heart. Her voice was rough silk, honest and unflinching.

"You know you're mine now."

His gaze darkened with reverence, his hand coming to cover hers.

"And you are mine, Sirati," he whispered, voice low and holy. "My Ashling. My spark. My fire. My first and final breath."

"What does Sirati mean?" she whispered in return.

"My desired path," he murmured. "My beautiful future."

Outside, the rain ran down the streets. The city exhaled in peace.

Inside, Roxy closed her eyes.

She had called for something real.

And he had come.

Not to take.

To stay.

***

The world outside still smoked in areas, but it was no longer choking.

In the days that followed the fire, the city recovered. Steam still occasionally hissed from storm grates. Streets shimmered with the lingering heat of the summer, but no longer threatened to melt. People came back out with sweat-streaked brows and wary hope.

When taking a break from the renovations, Roxy watched it happen from the doorway of *Veil and Ink*, a cold brew sweating in one hand and her Ifrit's warmth pressed into her back.

Love, it turned out, was not a lightning strike. It was a slow ignition. And once lit — it refused to die.

Today, Izan was barefoot in the shop's backroom, sleeves rolled to his elbows, wiring Raven's new coffee machine with the same quiet devotion as a man who once granted the wishes of gods — and now made espresso.

Roxy leaned against the doorframe, watching him work like it mattered — like espresso was sacred, and maybe it was.

"He's kind of handy to have around, ain't he?" Raven said, standing next to Roxy with a smile as they watched him work on the machine Raven had deemed the most important piece of equipment in the shop.

"Yes, I think I will keep him." Roxy returned her smile even wider.

His bronze skin caught the late afternoon light, and when he turned and caught Roxy watching him, he smiled.

Soft. Loving. Claimed.

She was about to walk toward him when the door chimed.

A man stepped into the shop. Nondescript. Average. A type of face your eyes skimmed past without registering. But if you examined him, his gaze was sharp. Too sharp. He looked around as if expecting someone to stop him.

"I'm looking for a book," he said mildly. "Old. Handwritten. Symbols, drawings. I'm almost certain I left it here."

Before Roxy could answer, Raven popped up from behind the counter with a triumphant grin, holding the weathered book with the Lurian Sigil etched into its spine. "This what you're after? Creeped me out, so I stowed it under the 'Do Not Touch' shelf."

The man took it with reverent care. "Yes. Thank you." His eyes lingered a little too long on Roxy's thigh, though the ink was hidden beneath her jeans.

Then he left.

Or tried to.

As he rounded the corner outside, he slowed.

Izan stood in the alley's mouth, arms folded, backlit by the lowering sun. His body shimmered with restrained heat and power, a golden haze bleeding from his skin.

The man stopped, a breath too short. "Despite that protective look on your face," he said. "I'll say you're welcome."

Izan tilted his head, eyes unreadable. "Don't flatter yourself. You gave me a door. She opened it."

A beat.

A breeze stirred the heat between them.

The man smirked. "So dramatic — just like a creature of fire. May I assume my debt is cleared?"

Izan took one step closer, just enough for the space to press in, the air to grow tight.

"You may. But if you ever come looking for mischief," he said, voice a low growl, "remember this: I burn hotter now."

The man's smile faltered — then curved again, sharp and knowing. "Message received."

He gave a small bow.

And he was gone, book tucked under his arm, vanishing into the dusk like a spell already broken.

The world felt quieter. Safer. Warmer.

Roxy leaned against the doorway, watching Izan as he turned back to the shop and met her gaze once more. No shadows between them now. No more running. No more denial.

No more loneliness.

Only the heat of a love that had survived its own firestorm.

I found something real, Roxy thought, her breath catching as he crossed the distance to her again, — *and it found me.*

He pulled her into his arms and kissed her like she was the only woman who would ever matter to him.

Because she was.

Behind them, the world steamed and hissed, reborn in love's wake.

~*Finis*

*The city cools, the fires fade — but in the northern wilds, something
feral wakes to the scent of a female's fear
... and falls in love.*

THANK YOU FOR READING!

DID YOU ENJOY THIS BOOK?

IF *WICKED FIRE* LEFT a mark on you, tell a friend — or three. And if you have a moment to spare, a review on Amazon or Goodreads helps keep the fire burning for indie authors like me. Your words are our fuel. Your support is our magic.

Want to see more by V. P. Nightshade?
Visit her Author Page on Amazon
  https://www.amazon.com/author/vpnightshade

AUTHOR BIOGRAPHY

V. P. NIGHTSHADE

V. P. NIGHTSHADE WRITES the kind of romance your mother warned you about—dark, delicious, and devastatingly emotional.

Author of supernatural sagas and steamy fantasy tales, she conjures vivid worlds of passion, peril, and power. From vampire courts and cursed kingdoms to alien warlords and ancient gods — where monsters love too deeply, heroes bleed beautifully, and forever comes with a price — her stories twist the knife between heat and heartbreak ... and make you beg for more.

Every page pulses with rich, sensual prose and sharp emotional tension. Her heroines are haunted and hungry for freedom. Her heroes are broken, brutal, and breathtaking. And her plots? Twisted vines of fate, prophecy, and sacrifice — where nothing is safe, not even love.

She writes from the shadows. And she writes for readers who aren't afraid to follow her there.

If you like your romance haunting, your monsters tender, and your heroes barely clinging to their sanity ... welcome to the Nightshade novels. You've been expected.

Publishing costs are always increasing! Please don't wait; buy her novels now before the price changes!

Visit her Amazon Author page at:

https://www.amazon.com/author/vpnightshade